BOOK 2: Intermediate

a splash of color

Dennis Alexander

Romantic and Contemporary Piano Solos Designed to Enhance an Awareness of Imagery in Performance

Teachers are always searching for pieces which will immediately attract the attention of their junior high and high school students. My own students at this age always enjoy learning through the use of imagery, and I frequently resort to the use of various colors in hopes of stretching their imaginations to new heights. Some of your students may possibly think of other colors when playing these pieces, and of course that is not only good, but it is encouraged! The important point is that the music creates a response; the student should feel inspired by both the music and the power of imagination. I hope that the music will bring many smiles to your students' faces and give them a sense of renewed enthusiasm for practicing the piano. Enjoy!

Dennis Alexander

This series is dedicated with love and appreciation to my parents.

Alfred

Alfred Music Publishing Co., Inc.
P.O. Box 10003
Van Nuys, CA 91410-0003
alfred.com

ISBN-10: 0-7390-0587-1

ISBN-13: 978-0-7390-0587-3

Cover Photo
Paints and Brushes: © istockphoto / VikZa

for Amy

turquoise

violetta

zinc pink

dark caramel

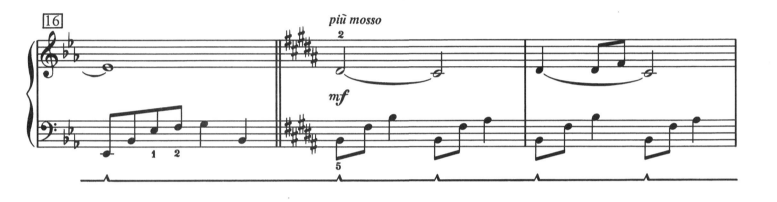

12

for Leigh
green tangerine

OPTIONAL ENDING *(may replace measures 49-56)*